The King's Trousers

By Robert Kraus

Illustrated by Fred Gwynne

Windmill Books/Simon & Schuster
New York

Text copyright © 1981 by Robert Kraus
Illustrations copyright © 1981 by Fred Gwynne
All rights reserved
including the right of reproduction
in whole or in part in any form
Published by Windmill Books, Inc. and
Simon & Schuster, a Division of Gulf & Western Corporation
Simon & Schuster Building
1230 Avenue of the Americas
New York, New York 10020
WINDMILL BOOKS and colophon are trademarks of Windmill Books, Inc.,
registered in the U.S. Patent and Trademark Office.
Manufactured in the United States of America
10 9 8 7 6 5 4 3 2 1

Library of Congress Cataloging in Publication Data

Kraus, Robert.
    The king's trousers.
    SUMMARY: When they discover that their proud and
haughty king puts on his trousers as they do, one leg
at a time, the angry villagers conclude that he is no
better than they are and decide to remove him from
the throne. & rulers
    [1. Kings, queens, rulers, etc.—Fiction.
2. Humorous stories]   I. Gwynne, Fred.
II. Title.
PZ7.K868Kg   [E]   79-14569

ISBN 0-671-42259-6

Once upon a time, in the Kingdom of Ethelbert, there lived a proud and haughty king. His name was King Ivor the Third.

"I am the greatest, noblest, finest king who ever lived!" proclaimed King Ivor.

And his loyal subjects and faithful toadies all agreed.

"Hail, hail, King Ivor the noble, the just, the magnificent!" they shouted. And they bowed down and groveled before him and scattered rose petals in his path.

"I am what everyone says and more," said King Ivor.

And he went to sleep in his cozy bed and stretched out on his satin sheets and dreamed about how wonderful he was.

In the morning, he leaped out of bed at the first cock's crow (being an early riser was one of his good qualities), slipped into his royal shirt, and put on his royal trousers.

Now on this particular morning, Bud, the Royal Window Washer, happened to be squeegeeing the royal bedroom windows. He saw King Ivor putting on his royal trousers, and he put them on just like everybody else, one leg at a time!

"Blimey!" exclaimed Bud.

And he jumped off his ladder (almost breaking his leg) and ran lickety-split into the village shouting, "The king puts on his trousers just like everyone else, one leg at a time! The king puts on his trousers just like everyone else, one leg at a time! The king puts on his trousers just like everyone else, one leg at a time!"

Now at this very moment, the villagers were getting out of their rumpled, uncomfortable beds (indeed, some of them did not have beds at all and slept on mats on the floor). Those of them who did not sleep in their clothes, a filthy habit indulged in by many, put on their trousers one leg at a time.

You can imagine their anger, not to mention rage, when they heard that the king put on his trousers just like everyone else, one leg at a time!

They were willing to put up with the king's vain, egotistical manner and mean, despotic ways; they were willing to toady and bow down to him if he were different and better than they were. But if he put on his trousers the same way that they did …

Their faces turned purple with rage.

Their eyes grew mean and darted hither and yon.

Their noses twitched angrily.

The villagers (many of whom at that very moment were putting on their own trousers) were so stunned to hear this startling news that many of them tripped in their own trouser legs and swayed this way and that, and many of them hopped around and around and toppled over.

"King Ivor puts on his trousers just like the rest of us!" they repeated over and over again until it became a mighty roar. They hopped, tripped, rolled, and spilled out onto the village green, and Slammo, the Pretender to the Throne, got up on his wife's shoulders and addressed the unruly mob.

"Since he puts on his trousers just like the rest of us, especially me, who is he to have such high and mighty ways? Who's to say he's not the Pretender to the Throne and I'm not the king?"

"Who indeed?" said his wife.

"Off with the king's head!" said Max the Butcher.

"Off with the king's pants!"
said Sam the Tailor.

"Let's storm the castle!" shouted the unruly mob.

Meanwhile, Satish the Baker, one of King Ivor's spies, harnessed his donkey and galloped lickety-split to the royal palace (on the pretext of delivering a rush order of cream puffs) to tell the king his secret was out.

"Your Majesty! Your Majesty!" cried Satish, prostrating himself before the king (an action King Ivor keenly enjoyed). "Your secret is out! Your secret is out! The whole village knows you put on your trousers just like everyone else. I fear they will attempt to remove you from the throne—"

"Let 'em eat cupcakes," said King Ivor.

"... and probably chop off your head," continued Satish.

"Let's think of a new way for me to get into my trousers— quickly," commanded King Ivor.

Before you could say "Slammo McJock," King Ivor slipped out of his trousers.

"Now hold these steady," he commanded Satish.

Satish held the king's trousers and the king
dove into them head first.

"Nice try, Ivor," said Satish.

The king tried as hard as he could to think of new ways to put on his trousers.
Sliding into his trousers.

Swimming into his trousers.

Having his trousers shot onto him.

Having his trousers dropped onto him.

Being juggled into his trousers.

Swinging into his trousers.

Jousted into his trousers.

Catapulted into his trousers.

He even thought of bulling his way into his trousers.

Then he climbed to the top of his canopied bed and leaped into his trousers with both legs.

The force of his landing split the royal trousers in two.
"There is no new way to get into my trousers," groaned
King Ivor.

Meanwhile, the angry mob, led by the Pretender to the Throne, was even now outside the castle gates, swimming across the royal moat, and scaling the royal walls while demanding the king's head. They charged up the royal stairs to the king's chamber chanting, "The king puts on his trousers just like everyone else, one leg at a time!"

They began breaking down the heavy, oak doors separating them from their despised monarch.

Meanwhile, inside the king's chamber, the yelling, the screaming for his head, the pounding on the oak doors gave the frantic king an inspired idea!

He clapped his hands twice and summoned the royal tailor, Sir Arthur of Prink, and his seven dwarves.

Then the king tore down the royal drapes and wrapped them around himself.

"Sew!" he commanded Sir Arthur and his seven dwarves.

Satish flung his body against the now splintering door.

But he could not prevent the entrance of the angry horde.
"You put your trousers on just like everyone else," they
screamed. "You're just as common as we are!"

"But I don't wear trousers," replied King Ivor. "I wear royal robes!"

"So he does," said Slammo McJock and his motley crew.

"Foiled again, said Slammo, and he led the deflated and defeated villagers back to the village.
And that is why kings wear royal robes.

Or so they say.

The End